With thanks to

**Horace Ové Faustin Charles Marilyn Smith
Gloria Cummins**

Errol Lloyd
NINI AT CARNIVAL

PUFFIN BOOKS

At last it was Carnival Day.
All the children were putting on
their costumes and helping
each other get ready.

Everybody was happy except Nini.
Nini didn't have a costume, you see.

And as the others marched
off to join the Carnival, Nini
just sat there and cried.

"If you don't stop crying this minute," said Nini's friend Betti, "I will turn you into an ugly frog."

"But if you come with me, I will make you Queen of the Carnival."

"Very funny," said Nini. "You're not a real fairy godmother and you haven't even got a magic wand."

"I might not be a real fairy godmother,"
said Betti, "but at Carnival there is
a lot of magic about."
So off they went to join the Carnival.

There was so much
noise and excitement.
There were horns and whistles
and flutes and drums, bottles and
bells and everything else.

Toot, toot! Tweet, tweet! Clang, clang! Bang, bang!
Katang, katang, katang, katang . . .

Everybody was having such a good time.
"If only I had a costume,"
whispered Nini to herself.

Then Nini suddenly heard:
"I am your fairy godmother from
the East. Put this on."

It was only a piece
of cloth, but it fitted
Nini perfectly.

"Now that you have a costume,"
said the fairy godmother,
"you are pretty enough to be
Queen of the Carnival."

Nini danced and danced
with happiness.

Soon everybody was dancing
with Nini, and everybody agreed
that Nini was the Queen
of the Carnival.

"Where have you been?"
said Nini to Betti.
"Look, I've been made
Queen of the Carnival."

"By a real fairy
godmother, I
suppose," said Betti.
"Yes," said Nini, "from the East
and with a real magic wand."
And Nini talked about it all the way home.

Some other Picture Puffins